This Notebook Belongs to:

Made in the USA
Monee, IL
14 February 2022

91275446R00069